Rev. Camden nodded slowly. It was just as he had thought. Lee had made up the story about his father being a high-powered private investigator. "I guess I was just trying to give Simon's friend the benefit of the doubt," the reverend said.

"The boy lied about his dad?" Sergeant Michaels asked.

Rev. Camden nodded. "Looks that way. I just wish I knew why."

Sergeant Michaels looked pensive. He opened his mouth, but then shut it again.

Rev. Camden glanced at him curiously. "What is it?"

"Well, it's probably nothing," Sergeant Michaels murmured.

"But?" Rev. Camden prompted him.

"I *do* know of a Jeff Patterson," Sergeant Michaels said.

Rev. Camden had a bad feeling about where this was headed. "And?" he prompted the sergeant.

"The Jeff Patterson I remember didn't work with the police," Sergeant Michaels said grimly. "But he was arrested by them."

Oh, boy, thought Rev. Camden. *This could get messy.*

7th Heaven™

THE PERFECT PLAN

By Amanda Christie

Based on the hit TV series
created by Brenda Hampton

And based on the following episode:

"With Honors"
Written by Sue Tenney

Random House 🏠 New York

www.randomhouse.com/kids

Library of Congress Catalog Card Number: 00-132048
ISBN: 0-375-80339-4

Printed in the United States of America
May 2000
10 9 8 7 6 5 4 3 2 1

CONTENTS

7th Heaven™

THE PERFECT PLAN

CHAPTER ONE

A BUSY NIGHT AT THE CAMDENS'

Rev. Camden was in his bedroom pulling a dirty diaper off David. At the same time, Mrs. Camden pulled a dirty diaper off Samuel. The twins, who were lying on the Camdens' bed, kicked their legs and made happy babbling noises.

Rev. Camden held David's diaper up in the air and made a face. "I bet mine's heavier than yours," he said to his wife.

Mrs. Camden held hers up, too. "Want to bet?" she said with a grin. "Mine must be at *least* twenty pounds."

Just then, Ruthie, the Camdens' youngest daughter, sauntered in. She had long, curly brown hair and big brown eyes. She was wearing jeans and a red sweatshirt and chomping on a wad of gum.

Ruthie glanced at her parents and then at her baby brothers. "The Olsens trained their puppy to go to the bathroom on newspaper," she stated wryly. "Think about it."

"Thanks, we'll keep that in mind," Rev. Camden said.

Ruthie plopped down on the bed next to her parents. "So," she said, blowing a big purple bubble. "What kind of fun stuff do you have planned for tomorrow?"

"Tomorrow?" Rev. Camden asked as he turned to his wife with a puzzled expression.

"It's a teacher-work day, Eric," Mrs. Camden explained. She picked up a fresh diaper and put it on Samuel. "Which means no school for Ruthie."

Ruthie pumped her fist triumphantly. "Yes! No school!"

Mrs. Camden smiled at her daughter. "I have a *great* plan for tomorrow. You can help me clean bathrooms, do laundry, repair the kitchen sink, darn socks, reorganize the linen closet…oh, yes…and go shopping."

"Toy shopping?" Ruthie said hopefully.

"*Food* shopping," Mrs. Camden corrected her.

Ruthie sighed dramatically. "Man, this is going to be *worse* than school." She jumped to her feet and headed for the door. "See you guys later. I think I'd better come up with my *own* plan for tomorrow."

Mrs. Camden grinned at Ruthie and then at her husband. Rev. Camden shook his head.

"What?" she asked him. "What's wrong?"

"Ruthie's right, Annie," Rev. Camden said in a mock-serious voice. "It *is* going to be worse than school." Just then, he caught sight of his oldest daughter, Mary, passing by the door. "Hey, you!" he called out cheerfully.

Mary stopped and poked her head in. She was tall and pretty, with an athletic build and long brown hair. She was dressed in jeans and a T-shirt.

"Hey, Mom. Hey, Dad. Need some help with those diapers?" she offered.

Rev. Camden fastened David's diaper, then tickled his tummy. David squealed happily. "No thanks, honey. We're all set. How're you doing?"

"Yes, how's the acceptance speech coming?" Mrs. Camden asked.

Mary was one of the star players on her high school varsity basketball team. She was receiving the senior "All Sports Award" from the local businessmen's association, along with her teammate Corey Conway. The awards assembly was the day after tomorrow, and she was in the middle of preparing her speech.

"Not great," Mary replied, shrugging. "But since Corey and I are sharing the award, maybe she can give the speech."

"Well, whoever gives the speech better choose her words very carefully," Rev. Camden advised. "It's not every day you win the local businessmen's senior 'All Sports Award.'"

Mary laughed. "Thanks a lot, Dad. I really wasn't feeling nervous enough as it is." Mary turned and continued down the hall. Rev. and Mrs. Camden were finishing up with the twins' diapers when Lucy, the Camdens' middle daughter, came rushing into the room. Lucy was shorter than Mary and had blondish brown hair that fell to her shoulders. She was dressed in jeans and a lacy red top. She flopped down on her parents' bed and fixed her big blue eyes on them.

"Mom, Dad, you *have* to help me," she

pleaded. "I don't want to work in the attendance office tomorrow…or the day after…or the day after that."

Mrs. Camden cocked her head. "Well, then maybe you shouldn't have volunteered?"

Lucy frowned. "But at the time I, um, 'volunteered,' I didn't realize I'd have to give up my study hall. I thought it would be before school or something, and I really need my study hall!"

"To study, right?" her father asked.

"Well, sure," Lucy replied, inspecting her nails. "Plus, it's the only time I have before lunch to catch up with my friends and retouch my makeup."

Her parents stared at her. "Catch up with your friends and retouch your makeup," her father repeated as if he couldn't believe his ears.

"Yes," Lucy said, very seriously. Noting their confused expressions, she said: "What? You're not going to help me?"

David began to squirm and whimper. Samuel soon did the same. Rev. and Mrs. Camden then each picked up a baby and headed for the door. "You'll be fine, honey," Mrs. Camden called over her shoulder.

Lucy sighed and flopped back on the bed. "They just don't understand," she mumbled to herself.

"Do you want to feed the babies or start dinner?" Mrs. Camden asked her husband as they headed down the hallway.

"Why don't I do dinner tonight? I'm feeling inspired," Rev. Camden replied, shifting David from one arm to the other. "Let's think...take-out pizza or take-out Mexican?"

Happy, the family dog, came bounding out of Simon's room and cut in front of the Camdens. She jumped up and pawed Rev. Camden's leg.

"Hey, girl," Rev. Camden said, patting Happy on the head. Happy's fluffy white tail wagged back and forth.

Simon emerged from his room. He was thirteen years old and had short blond hair and blue eyes. Just behind him was a boy with long black hair, dressed in faded khakis and a hooded sweatshirt.

"Hi, Mom. Hi, Dad. Can Lee stay over for dinner?" Simon said, stuffing his hands into the pockets of his jeans.

"Sure. Hi, Lee," Mrs. Camden said with a smile. "Just call your mom and let her know where you are, okay?"

Lee's eyes dropped to the floor. "Um, my mom died a long time ago, Mrs. Camden," he said.

Rev. and Mrs. Camden exchanged a quick glance. "I'm sorry," Mrs. Camden said, touching Lee's elbow. "We didn't know."

Lee shrugged. "It's okay. She died when I was a baby. I don't really remember her."

"What about your dad?" Rev. Camden asked.

"He works nights," Lee replied.

Mrs. Camden frowned. "Who usually feeds you?"

"My grandma," Lee said.

"Why don't you call her, then?" Mrs. Camden suggested.

Lee nodded. "Okay."

"Hey, Lee!" Simon said excitedly. "Tell them what your dad does." Before Lee could speak, Simon turned to his parents and blurted out, "His father is a *private investigator*. He works with the local police *and* the FBI. The FBI, that is *so* cool."

"Yes, very cool," Rev. Camden agreed.

Simon slapped Lee on the back. Lee grinned at him. "Come on, let's go call your grandma," Simon said.

The two boys raced downstairs, followed by Happy. Mrs. Camden leaned against her husband and smiled sweetly at him. "Well, I think being a minister is cooler than working with the FBI," she said.

He kissed her on the cheek. "And that's why I think you're the bomb, baby," he joked.

The Crawford University library was more crowded than usual. The Camdens' oldest son, Matt, and his girlfriend, Shana, had to look around for a while before they found a table. Matt was tall and good-looking, with longish brown hair. Shana was petite, with short blond hair.

Tomorrow there was a killer American History midterm. Even though Matt and Shana were in pretty good shape for it, they still had more studying to do.

Shana sat down at the table and smiled up at Matt. He smiled back. They had been dating for a long time now. Matt felt really lucky to have such a wonderful, pretty, smart, and fun-to-be-with girlfriend like Shana.

Matt sat across from her, plunked his backpack down, and started pulling out some books.

A piece of paper fluttered out. Matt quickly picked it up. It was the honor code that Professor Valentine, their American History teacher, had made all the students sign.

Matt held it out to Shana. "This honor code is so confusing," he complained. He kept his voice low so the other students wouldn't be bothered. "I still don't understand it."

Shana pulled a couple of books out of her backpack. "What's not to understand? It's pretty simple—when taking a test, don't cheat. And if you see someone cheat, turn them in."

"Hey, you guys!" a voice suddenly interrupted them.

Matt glanced up. James Potter, a student in their American History class, walked toward them. He was dressed in jeans, a button-down shirt, and an expensive-looking black leather jacket.

James stopped at their table and smiled at Matt and Shana. "Hey, what's happening?"

"Not much," Matt replied, noticing that Shana did not say hi to James.

James didn't seem to notice, though. His eyes were fixed on Matt. "Hey, Camden. Listen, I am *so* glad I ran into you. I need someone to help me cram for the American History midterm, and I heard you tutor for money."

"Uh, James? The test is tomorrow," Matt replied.

"And Matt already has a job," Shana said, glancing pointedly at Matt.

James clasped his hands together and bowed his head. "Please, Camden. I'm desperate. Name your price...money is not a problem."

Matt felt torn. On one hand, it seemed like a waste of time to help James. After all, the test was tomorrow—how much could he really teach him by then? But on the other hand, James really did seem desperate. "I'd like to help," Matt said finally. "But—"

"Puh-leeeze," James begged. "I'm going to fail! How can you sit there and just let me fail?"

Shana gave Matt a look, but he couldn't decipher it. He frowned at Shana and mouthed, *What?*

Shana said nothing. Finally, Matt turned to James and sighed. "Okay. I'll meet you back here same time tomorrow." He added, "But I'm not making any promises."

James clasped Matt on the shoulder. "Man, you are a life saver. I'll see you *mañana*."

As James walked off, Matt saw that Shana was really glaring at him.

"What?" he said to her. "Do you have a problem with James Potter or something?"

Shana crossed her arms over her chest. "He cheats," she said matter-of-factly.

CHAPTER TWO

RUTHIE'S DAY OFF

The following morning, Ruthie lay curled up on the living room sofa. Luckily for her, her mother seemed to have forgotten about cleaning bathrooms and doing laundry and all that other boring stuff. In fact, Ruthie had found a much more interesting way to spend her day off. She was channel-surfing, munching on a bowl of buttery popcorn, and drinking a big glass of milk with her favorite weird curly straw.

She held up the remote control: *click, click, click.* A series of images quickly flashed across the TV screen. There was a cartoon cat chasing a cartoon mouse. There was an ad for a new perfume called *Fabulous!* There was a reporter standing in front of a burning skyscraper. Then one of the images caught Ruthie's attention, so she stopped clicking. There was a woman in a fancy-looking kitchen who was speaking into a walkie-talkie to a boy about Ruthie's age. The boy, who was playing in some park with a bunch of kids, was speaking into a walkie-talkie, too.

> The Boy: *Hi, Mom. I'm at the park.*
> The Mother: *It's time to come home, Danny.*
> *Dinner's almost ready!*
> The Boy: *I'll be right home. Over and out!*

The screen split into two scenes and then froze. Ruthie stared, mesmerized, at the side-by-side images of Danny and his mom smiling into their walkie-talkies. Then a man's voice came out of nowhere and boomed: "Don't find yourself out of touch with your loved ones! You, too, can get the new, state-of-the-art Yakalot II Walkie-Talkies. Only twenty-nine ninety-nine plus shipping and handling. And if you order now, you can get a free imitation-silver pocket calculator…"

"That's *it!*" Ruthie said to herself.

She stuffed a handful of popcorn into her

mouth and clicked the TV off. She got up and ran into the kitchen.

Mrs. Camden was feeding the twins. Well, at least she was *trying* to feed them. The boys were sitting side by side in their baby chairs and were throwing bagel bits onto the floor and dribbling apple sauce all over themselves. Rev. Camden was at the sink, finishing up the breakfast dishes.

"How's your day off going so far?" Mrs. Camden asked Ruthie, tearing a bagel in half.

"Great!" Ruthie said. "Listen. Can I have twenty-nine dollars and ninety-nine cents?"

Her father raised an eyebrow. "What for?"

"I just *have* to have these walkie-talkies I saw on TV," Ruthie explained.

"Walkie-talkies," Mrs. Camden repeated. She spooned some apple sauce into David's mouth. David sputtered, and apple sauce flew everywhere. "Now, why on Earth would you need walkie-talkies, Ruthie?" Mrs. Camden asked, reaching for a towel.

"So I can call all my friends, and they can call me back," Ruthie explained. "And it'll only cost twenty-nine dollars and ninety-nine cents."

"But if you use the phone to call your friends and pretend the phone is a walkie-talkie, then it'll cost less," Mrs. Camden pointed out.

"Makes sense to me," Rev. Camden agreed.

Ruthie rolled her eyes. "Parents!" she said in exasperation. She turned around and walked out of the kitchen.

After Ruthie left, Rev. Camden turned to his wife and said, "What exactly *is* a teacher-work day?"

Mrs. Camden thought for a moment, then said: "A parents-work-*harder* day?"

Simon stuffed a bunch of books into his locker. The bell was about to ring, and the main hallway of the junior high school was bustling with kids. Next to him, Lee was taking some books out of the bottom of his locker and cramming them into his backpack.

Simon turned to Lee. "So, is your dad working with the police again tonight?"

Lee shrugged. "Yeah."

Simon thought for a moment. "Okay, so then why don't you come over to my house again?" he suggested.

Lee had stayed for pizza the night before at the Camdens' house. Afterward, they'd hung out in Simon's room, studying and having a fun time. Lee was a good friend, and Simon liked having him around. It seemed Lee enjoyed being at the Camdens' house, too.

Lee grinned. "Sure, that'd be great."

"Your father works a lot, huh?" Simon said, slinging his backpack over his shoulder.

"Less than when he worked for NASA," Lee replied.

"NASA, as in the space program NASA?" Simon asked in amazement.

Lee nodded. "Yeah."

Simon shook his head in disbelief. "The police...NASA...and the FBI. Your dad is the coolest!"

"Yeah, he's cool," Lee said. He closed his locker and grinned at Simon. "I'm lucky he's my dad."

Over at the high school, Mary was at her locker. She was talking to Corey Conway. Corey was short and blond and full of energy. She was also one of the best basketball players Mary had ever been on a team with.

The two girls were trying to figure out what to do about the awards assembly. They still hadn't figured out their acceptance speech. In fact, they didn't even have a first sentence!

Mary sighed. "I have *no* idea what to say," she complained to Corey.

"I know," Corey said. "Who would have thought that winning an award could be this much trouble?"

Mary laughed.

Just then, a girl named Elaine came up to them. Elaine was on the basketball team with Mary and Corey. There was a tall, red-haired girl with her who Mary didn't recognize.

"Hey, Elaine," Mary said.

Elaine smiled. "Hey, you guys—this is Maggie. The coach asked me to show her around. She's a new transfer student from Washington High."

Mary and Corey both shook hands with Maggie. Maggie's gaze lingered on Corey for a long moment.

Corey smiled uncertainly at Maggie. "Um, can I help you?"

Maggie shook her head. "I'm sorry. You just...well, you look like someone I knew at Lincoln Junior High."

Corey's smile faded. "I've never been to Lincoln," she said, a little abruptly.

"Sorry, my mistake," Maggie said.

Corey glanced at Mary and then at the other girls. "Better get to class," she murmured. "See you guys later," she said as she quickly shut her locker and walked off.

"Hey, Corey! We still need to talk about our speech!" Mary called after her. But Corey didn't seem to hear. *I wonder if she's OK?* Mary thought.

Sunlight streamed through the windows of the Crawford University library. Matt leaned back in his chair and drummed his fingers impatiently on the tabletop. His American History textbook was open to Chapter One, and he was ready to go. He was…but James Potter wasn't.

James had made a big deal out of wanting Matt to tutor him, so Matt had shown up for their tutoring session right on time. James, however, had been ten minutes late. And now he was hanging out at a table across the room, flirting with two girls.

What is up with him? Matt wondered impatiently.

Matt saw Shana enter the library. He waved at her. Shana waved back and walked up to his table. She glanced at him and immediately said, "What's wrong?"

Matt pointed to James, across the room. "This tutoring is a waste of my time and his money," Matt declared.

Shana stared at James. "James doesn't care about money."

Matt chuckled dryly. "Everybody cares about money."

"Not when your father is Roy Potter," Shana pointed out.

"Roy Potter?" Matt repeated. He was totally confused. "Who's Roy Potter?"

Shana made a face. "Roy Potter, as in Potter Library, Potter Hospital, Potter Pavilion, Potter Center...Potter everything."

"Oh, *that* Roy Potter." Matt couldn't believe it. He had never made the connection between James Potter and the famous Potter name, which was all over Glenoak.

"James's dad is loaded," Shana went on. "And James is a spoiled rich kid living off his dad and his trust fund. Crawford is the third school his dad has *bought* him into."

She glanced across the room at James, who was still flirting with the two cute girls. "The only thing James Potter wants to learn is the fastest way to open a pony keg."

CHAPTER THREE

THE BIG RUMOR

Rev. Camden was sitting in a rocking chair in the twins' room. David was cradled in his right arm, Samuel in his left. He had just finished strolling them around the neighborhood. Now the boys were settling down for their morning nap.

Rev. Camden rocked back and forth and hummed softly to them. His own eyelids were beginning to droop a little. It seemed as though he could never get enough sleep these days.

"Hi, Daddy!"

The reverend's eyes immediately snapped back open. Ruthie was standing in the doorway. She glanced at her brothers, who were now fast asleep.

Rev. Camden got up carefully and put the

boys in their cribs. He then turned to Ruthie. "Hi, honey," he said, rubbing his eyes and stretching his back. "What's up?"

Ruthie walked up to him and smiled very sweetly. "The twins are *so* lucky that you're their daddy," she said. "I'm lucky you're my daddy, too. I love you!"

Rev. Camden nodded. He knew this tactic all too well. "Listen, Ruthie. I think you should get the walkie-talkies you want…" he began.

Ruthie let out a little squeal of delight. And then she grabbed her father and hugged him fiercely. "You're the best dad ever," she mumbled into his shirt.

"And I also think you're old enough to earn the money yourself," the reverend finished.

Ruthie pulled away abruptly. She gave him a look. "I hope you're not suggesting that 'allowance' thing that the other kids do."

Rev. Camden nodded. "You can take out the trash for three dollars a week," he told her. "If you really want those walkie-talkies, that's the deal. Take it or leave it."

Ruthie headed for the door. "I'll leave it. There are much easier ways to make money than by working."

Rev. Camden watched her go, then turned to the sleeping twins. "Don't be in a hurry to start talking, okay?" he whispered to them.

Okay, I'd rather be anywhere but here, Lucy said to herself. *Even Trig class would be better than this.*

Lucy was sitting in the attendance office at a desk with stacks and stacks of papers in front of her. And all the while, her friends were in study hall, hanging out and catching up on the gossip and having lots of fun—*without* her.

Lucy glared at the mountains of papers. What was she supposed to do with them, anyway? She reached over to pick up one of the stacks...and a small, sharp pain shot through her hand.

"Ow!" she cried out. She dropped the papers and inspected her hand. There was a thin line of blood.

"Great, a paper cut," she moaned, sucking on her hand. "Just what I needed."

"Excuse me. Lucy Camden?"

Lucy glanced up, startled. She dropped her hand to her lap. Standing before her was a tall, gorgeous blond guy. Lucy paused for a moment and then realized it was Tyler Smith. Tyler "Adonis of Glenoak High" Smith, as everyone at school knew him.

How does he know me? she thought.

Lucy sat up a little straighter and stared at him. "How'd you know my name?" she asked him curiously.

"It's on your shirt," Tyler said.

Lucy looked down. She'd forgotten that she was wearing a name badge.

"Oh," she said, smiling at him. He smiled back. He had a perfect smile. *I could get used to this attendance thing,* Lucy thought.

"I need a hall pass," Tyler said after a moment.

Lucy was still smiling at him.

"Um, I'm late," Tyler prompted her.

"What? Oh, yeah…right. Sure," Lucy mumbled. She reached over for a pad and pen and began to write a pass for him. Then she hesitated.

"I'm sorry," Lucy said apologetically. "I need an excuse. For the pass, I mean." She added, "It's the rules."

Tyler leaned forward and smiled that perfect smile at her again. Lucy felt her insides melting.

"What are my choices?" Tyler asked her lazily.

Lucy leaned back and chewed on the tip of her pen. "Well, let's see. How about sickness?" she suggested.

Tyler nodded. "Sickness sounds good."

"Are you sick?" Lucy asked him.

"Not anymore," Tyler replied.

As Lucy wrote out the pass, she thought, *This is the best volunteer job in the whole world...*

Mary was sitting in study hall, reading over her book of Shakespeare's plays. She had to get ready for a quiz on *Hamlet*, but all she could think about was the awards assembly tomorrow—and the speech that she still didn't have.

Picking up a pen, she wrote: *We'd like to thank the businessmen's association for this honor.*

She crossed that out and wrote under it: *We're very honored that the businessmen's association chose to honor us with this honor.*

"No!" she muttered to herself, crossing that out. "Too many 'honors'!"

Just then, she felt a tap on her shoulder. She turned around. It was Elaine.

"Hey, Elaine," Mary said, closing her notebook. "What's up?"

Elaine knelt down and leaned close to Mary. Her eyes were gleaming.

"Did you hear the rumor?" Elaine said excitedly. "It's all over school!"

Mary grinned. "I just saw you this morning. How can anything be all over school?"

"What can I say? The really juicy stuff has a life of its own." Elaine leaned even closer and lowered her voice. "Corey Conway had a baby when she was fourteen," she announced dramatically.

Mary's jaw dropped. She couldn't believe it. "C-Corey?" she said after a moment. "Had a baby?" She shook her head. "No way!"

Elaine nodded vigorously. "Yeah. Maggie, the new girl, said there was a Corey Conway who went to her junior high school. And *that* Corey got pregnant and dropped out of school to have a baby."

Mary shook her head again. She thought about the Corey she knew. Corey the basketball player. Corey the straight-A student. *There's no way.*

"Look," Mary said out loud to Elaine.

"You've known Maggie for three hours. You've known Corey for three *years*. You're listening to Maggie?"

"Maggie's story sounded pretty convincing," Elaine replied.

"Don't get swept up in rumor fever," Mary warned her as she suddenly caught sight of Corey walking into the room.

Mary was about to warn Elaine to shut up, but before she had the chance, Elaine stood up and blurted, "I'm telling you, I think it's totally believable that Corey Conway had a baby!"

Corey froze in her tracks. *She overheard,* Mary thought, her heart sinking. She stared helplessly at Corey and then glared at Elaine.

"What?" Elaine said, confused. *"What?"*

Mary stood up and pointed to Corey. Elaine turned around.

Elaine turned beet red. "Oh, hey, Corey!" she said, a little too cheerfully. "Uh, what's new?"

Corey just shook her head. She looked really upset. Then she turned on her heels and ran out of the room.

"Sorry," Elaine said to Mary, shrugging. Mary didn't reply. She picked up her stuff and ran out of the room after Corey.

CHAPTER FOUR

THE TRUTH COMES OUT

"Okay, so, what's the Tweed Ring?" Matt asked James Potter.

James leaned back in his chair. "The Tweed Ring," he repeated slowly. "That's the, uh... the...you know, that *thing*. The thing that...has to do with...jewel robbers who wore...uh, tweed."

Matt sighed. James wasn't anywhere near ready for the American History exam. And unfortunately, the exam was that afternoon.

They had spent the last two hours in the library, studying. Although "studying" was a generous way to describe it. Matt had finally gotten James to tear himself away from the two girls and sit down at the table with him. But then James kept getting up to make phone calls. And to check his e-mail. And to talk to more girls.

All in all, they had probably gotten about ten minutes' worth of studying done, Matt guessed.

"The Tweed Ring was a gang of crooked New York City politicians in the 1800s," Matt corrected James. He turned the page of the American History textbook. "Okay, how about this one? Who was president during the Teapot Dome scandal?"

"Oh, yeah, that," James said, lacing his fingers together. "*That* is a piece of cake. One of those Roosevelt guys! You know, Teddy, Freddy, Eddie, whatever."

"Warren Harding, actually," Matt said.

James sighed and reached for his backpack. "Tweed this, Teapot that...Listen, Camden, what do you say we wrap this up?" he suggested. "If I don't know it by now, I'm never going to know it."

"No problem," Matt said. He started stuffing his books and notebooks into his backpack. James was right. If he didn't know it by now, he *was* never going to know it.

"Thanks for the help," James told him.

"I don't know why you're thanking me," Matt said, shrugging. "I didn't really do anything. Not that I didn't try," he added.

James grinned sheepishly. "I know I have a problem focusing on schoolwork."

"But on the up side, you have no problem focusing on women." Matt nodded his head at two *new* girls who were staring and smiling at James. James smiled back at them.

And then, as if remembering suddenly, James reached into his pocket for his wallet. He took out a wad of money and handed it to Matt.

Matt took the money and counted it. Then he counted it again. He realized it was way too much.

"I think you overpaid me," Matt said, taking half the bills and trying to give them back to James. But James held his hand up to stop him.

"W-What are you doing?" Matt said, confused.

James leaned forward slightly. "Maybe you could *earn* the extra money," he said, lowering his voice.

Matt frowned. "Earn it...how?"

"The only way I'm going to pass the history midterm is if someone else takes it for me," James explained. "And you could use some money. So..." He raised his eyebrows, waiting for Matt's answer.

Matt couldn't believe what he was hearing. "Are...are you asking me to help you *cheat?*"

"'Cheat' is such a harsh word," James said lightly. "I prefer 'assist,'" he said, smiling at Matt.

Matt stared at him, not knowing what to say.

Rev. Camden paused in the living room and listened.

Silence.

Silence was a rare sound in the Camden household. Of course, the twins were still napping. His wife was out doing some errands. Mary, Lucy, and Simon were in school. And Ruthie was up in her room with Happy, being very, well...*silent*. He wasn't sure what she was up to, but she seemed to be hatching some sort of plan to get her walkie-talkies. In any case, she hadn't come back to him with any new and improved requests for the money.

Rev. Camden sighed. As much as he enjoyed the peace and quiet, there was something weighing on his mind. A nagging question he had about Simon's friend Lee. A question he hoped would be cleared up momentarily.

The doorbell rang. "There he is," Rev. Camden said to himself, heading for the front door.

It was Sergeant Michaels, just as the reverend had expected. "Hello, Sergeant," Rev. Camden said, opening the door to let him in. "I'm glad you stopped by."

Sergeant Michaels stepped into the foyer. "Yes, I got your message. What can I do for you?"

Rev. Camden closed the door and turned to Sergeant Michaels. "I wanted to ask you about Jeff Patterson," he began.

"Jeff Patterson," Sergeant Michaels repeated. He looked a little confused.

"He's a private investigator," Rev. Camden explained. "His son Lee told us that his father works with the Glenoak Police Department. As a matter of fact, he's supposedly working on a case with you right now."

Sergeant Michaels shook his head. "The

police have detectives for detective work. We don't hire outside help."

Rev. Camden nodded slowly. It was just as he had thought. Lee had made up the story about his father being a high-powered private investigator. "I guess I was just trying to give Simon's friend the benefit of the doubt," the reverend said.

"The boy lied about his dad?" Sergeant Michaels asked.

Rev. Camden nodded. "Looks that way. I just wish I knew why."

Sergeant Michaels looked pensive. He opened his mouth but then shut it again.

Rev. Camden glanced at him curiously. "What is it?"

"Well, it's probably nothing," Sergeant Michaels murmured.

"But?" Rev. Camden prompted him.

"I *do* know of a Jeff Patterson," Sergeant Michaels said.

Rev. Camden had a bad feeling about where this was headed. "And?" he prompted the sergeant.

"The Jeff Patterson I remember didn't work with the police," Sergeant Michaels said grimly.

"But he was arrested by them."

Oh, boy, thought Rev. Camden. *This could get messy.*

CHAPTER FIVE

MEETING BERNADETTE

Simon sat at his desk, finishing up his algebra homework. Most of his friends hated algebra, but Simon really liked it. He thought numbers were very neat, orderly, and methodical. They never surprised you or did things that you didn't expect them to do.

Happy was curled up in a ball at his feet. She was snoring softly, and her tail was thumping rhythmically against the floor: *thump, thump, thump.*

5x times 6y equals what? Simon quickly wrote down the answer. He wanted to get his work done before Lee came over for dinner. Afterward, Simon figured that the two of them would check out his new video game. Or maybe Lee could tell him more stories about his dad's experiences with the FBI and NASA…

"Helloooo!"

Simon glanced up. Ruthie was standing in the doorway, grinning from ear to ear.

He sighed. "What do you want?"

Ruthie walked into the room and leaned against his desk. "I'll make this quick. I need twenty-nine dollars and ninety-nine cents," she announced.

On the floor, Happy stirred. She opened one eye and regarded Ruthie.

Simon laughed. "I am *not* giving you any money," he told his sister.

"I'll pay you back," Ruthie promised.

Simon put his pencil down. "Careful, Pinocchio, your nose is growing."

"Hey!" Ruthie protested.

"'Hey' what? You never pay money back to the people who are crazy enough to lend it to you," Simon pointed out.

Ruthie frowned. She plucked at the hem of her sweater. "Come on, Simon. There must be *something* I can do to get you to loan me the money."

Simon thought for a moment. "I'll tell you

what," he said. "If you can get someone to mow the lawn for me on Saturday, I'll consider loaning you the money."

Ruthie beamed. She turned and headed for the door. "I'll be back."

"Take all the time you need," Simon called after her. "You're going to need it! I've already asked everyone in the house."

Ruthie paused at the door and grinned. "Yeah, but you aren't *me*," she said as she pranced down the hall.

Simon rolled his eyes, then glanced down at Happy. "What do you think, girl?"

Happy barked.

"I couldn't agree more," Simon told her.

In the kitchen, Mrs. Camden was folding a stack of laundry. She'd lost track of how many loads she'd done today. With a family of nine, including two babies, it seemed as though the washer and drier were going all the time.

She paused, picked up her mug, and took a sip of tea. *Mmm, cinnamon.* The smell of it filled the kitchen, along with the equally pleasant smells of fabric softener and the oatmeal cookies baking in the oven.

Rev. Camden came into the kitchen. He looked concerned.

"Eric? What's wrong?" Mrs. Camden asked him.

"Hmm? Oh, I'll tell you about it later." He glanced at the laundry she was folding. "Matt's?"

Mrs. Camden nodded. "How come kids always want to leave the nest, but their laundry wants to stay?" she asked him.

Her husband smiled at her. Just then, Lucy strolled into the kitchen. She looked as though she were walking on air.

Mrs. Camden raised her eyebrows. "How was the attendance office?" she asked her.

Lucy went to the refrigerator and poured herself a glass of milk. "Oh, it was fabulous, fun, fantastic..." she raved. She closed the refrigerator door, gave them a radiant smile, and floated back out of the kitchen, milk in hand.

The Camdens exchanged a glance. "Teenagers," Mrs. Camden said simply.

"Yeah, if you don't like their mood, wait ten minutes," Rev. Camden remarked.

Ruthie came in just as Lucy was leaving.

She made a beeline for the refrigerator. "Hi, guys!" she called out.

"So," Rev. Camden said. "Have you reconsidered my offer? If you really want those walkie-talkies, getting an allowance is the only way to go."

Ruthie grabbed some grapes from the refrigerator. "No, thank you," she said, popping a grape into her mouth. "I have a plan. And it's a lot easier than taking out the trash for the rest of my life." Ruthie then popped some more grapes into her mouth and headed upstairs. Mrs. Camden turned to her husband with a worried expression.

"She has a plan. Should we be concerned?" she asked him.

"Not concerned," Rev. Camden corrected her. "Afraid. *Very* afraid."

Matt walked into the American History classroom and looked around for Shana. He spotted her and waved. She waved back. Unfortunately, all the seats near her were taken.

He found a seat near the front of the class. Out of the corner of his eye, he saw that Professor Valentine was starting to pass out the exams. Fortunately, Matt felt really prepared. Unlike James Potter, who was anything *but* prepared.

At that moment, James ambled into the room. He slid into the seat next to Matt and set his backpack on the floor.

Oh, great, Matt thought.

James leaned toward him. "Hey, Matt. What's new?" he said easily.

"I told you when I gave your money back, I am *not* helping you cheat," Matt whispered fiercely.

"Is there a problem here, Mr. Camden?" Matt glanced up quickly. Professor Valentine was standing there, exams in hand.

Matt shook his head. "There's no problem," he said, looking pointedly at James.

Professor Valentine didn't say anything. He put a copy of the exam upside-down on Matt's desk, then proceeded down the row.

Matt saw that James was still leaning in his direction. "Move *away*," Matt warned.

"Relax, Camden," James murmured. "I don't need you. I made other plans."

James tapped the shoulder of a blond guy sitting in front of him. The guy turned around.

He and James smiled meaningfully at each other.

"You're not the only guy on campus who needs money," James told Matt in a low voice.

"Mr. Camden! Mr. Potter! No talking!" Professor Valentine called out from the back of the room.

Matt whirled around. He smiled nervously at Professor Valentine. *Great,* he thought. *James is getting me in trouble, and I'm not even doing anything.*

Professor Valentine finished passing out the exams and then moved to the front of the room. "Okay. All books, backpacks, and purses on the floor," he ordered.

The students put their stuff under their desks. After a moment, Professor Valentine said, "Everyone may turn over the exam and begin."

Matt turned his exam over. He was really feeling uncomfortable about what James Potter was about to do. He glanced over his shoulder briefly and caught Shana's eye. She mouthed the words: *What's wrong?*

"Face the front, Mr. Camden," Professor

Valentine snapped. He sounded really irritated now.

Matt nodded and turned around. Picking up his pen, he hunched down and tried to focus on the exam.

After a few minutes, Professor Valentine left the room. The blond guy in front of James moved his exam way to the right. James leaned forward, looked over the guy's shoulder, and began copying his answers like mad.

Matt sank down in his seat. What was it the honor code said? *When taking a test, don't cheat. And if you see someone cheat, turn them in.*

The words kept echoing in his head.

Mary walked up the sidewalk toward Corey's house. She hoped she was doing the right thing by going there. She had tried to chase Corey down after the incident in study hall with Elaine. But Corey had taken off, and Mary hadn't been able to find her.

I've got to talk to her, Mary thought.

She reached a brown stucco house and checked the address. *Yup, that's the one,* she told herself. Now that she thought of it, she realized she had never been to Corey's house before—not in the three years that she'd known her.

A little blond girl was riding a tricycle in the driveway. She looked as though she was about four years old.

"Hi," the little girl called out.

"Hi," Mary replied.

"My name's Bernadette," the girl said. "What's yours?"

Mary told her. "Is your mommy home?"

The front door opened, and Corey stepped out. She smiled sweetly at Bernadette. "Go inside, honey."

Bernadette waved to Mary. "Bye!"

"Bye, Bernadette," Mary said, waving back.

Bernadette scrambled off her tricycle and skipped into the house. Mary and Corey stared at each other.

"Is that who I think it is?" Mary finally said.

Corey nodded. Her eyes never left Mary's. "Yeah, she's my daughter. Maggie wasn't lying. The rumor is true."

Mary swallowed. It was true, but it was still so hard to believe, even after seeing Bernadette in person.

Corey started to go back inside. "Well, now that you've seen her, you can go," she said, her voice full of bitterness.

Mary rushed forward and grabbed Corey's arm. "You're not going anywhere until we talk. I looked for you at school, but you disappeared."

"I had a baby when I was fourteen. Are you satisfied now?" Corey snapped.

Mary hesitated. She wanted Corey to know that she was on her side, one hundred percent. But her feelings were all in a jumble, and she had no idea how to put them into words.

After a moment, Mary said, "How did you hide this from everyone?"

"It wasn't easy," Corey said, bowing her head. "I couldn't have anyone over to my house. I couldn't go to parties or stay out late. And forget about dating. With taking care of a baby, I barely had time to go to school and play basketball."

She gazed off into the distance. "When I think about it, I actually don't know how I was able to finish high school," she murmured. "Most teen mothers don't. But I do know that I couldn't have done it without my mom. She's been there for me every step of the way…since the day I told her I was pregnant."

Mary shook her head. "Man. I thought being hit by a car was hard. But motherhood at fourteen…"

Corey gazed at Mary. "You know what's harder than motherhood?"

"What?" Mary asked her.

"Your friends talking and whispering behind your back," Corey said. Mary could see that her eyes were shiny with tears.

Mary put her hand on Corey's arm. "Not everyone is talking about you."

"Oh, please!" Corey exclaimed. "This spring, I'm graduating *magna cum laude*. I'm a top scorer on a championship basketball team. And I've been accepted to three Ivy League universities." She added, "But now, thanks to that new girl Maggie, the only thing anyone cares about is that I had a baby at fourteen."

With that, Corey burst into tears. Trying to fight back her own tears, Mary reached out and hugged her friend. *I have to help her,* Mary thought desperately. *But how?*

CHAPTER SIX

ACCUSATION

The doorbell rang. Lucy plunked her glass of milk down on the counter and ran to the foyer. *I wonder who that could be?* she thought. *I hope it's for me.*

Even if the doorbell wasn't for her—or even if it was some annoying door-to-door salesman—Lucy wouldn't care. Nothing could touch her incredibly good mood. Tyler Smith had drifted into her orbit. Tyler Smith had smiled his perfect smile at her.

Lucy opened the door. Her heart practically stopped.

Standing there was *Tyler Smith*, in the flesh.

"Tyler," she managed to say after she'd recovered the ability to speak. "W-what are you doing here?"

Tyler put one hand against the doorway and leaned into it. "Do you have a date yet for the Fall Fling dance?" he asked her.

Where is he going with this? Lucy wondered. "Uh, no," she said tentatively.

Tyler beamed. "Well, now you do."

"I do?" Lucy was totally confused.

Tyler nodded.

And then it dawned on her. "*You* want to take *me* to the dance?" she gasped.

Tyler nodded again.

Lucy was about to scream *"Yes!"* when something suddenly occurred to her. Something about another girl Tyler was dating. *Oh, yes, Courtney Webber. That's her name,* Lucy remembered. She'd heard the rumor way back but had not paid much attention to it.

"Um, I thought you were dating Courtney Webber," Lucy said.

Tyler shook his head. "Yeah, we were dating, but we broke up. So what do you say?"

"We broke up"—the most beautiful words in the English language, thought Lucy.

"I guess you've got yourself a date then," Lucy told him happily.

Tyler smiled his perfect smile at her. And

then he leaned over and kissed her on the cheek. The briefest little kiss, and yet it was like his smile—*perfect*.

Lucy thought, *If I faint now, I wonder if he'll notice…*

Matt joined the throng of students shuffling out of Professor Valentine's class. He knew that he had done well on the midterm, but he was feeling tense from the James Potter situation.

Once he got in the hallway, he spotted Shana and headed straight for her. He grabbed her arm. "Hey, Shana."

Shana looked at him in concern. "Are you okay? What's going on? Does it have something to do with James?"

Matt started to reply. But then Professor Valentine came up to him. Noting his expression, Matt thought: *Uh-oh, he doesn't look happy.*

Professor Valentine stopped in front of Matt and Shana. He peered at Matt over the top of his glasses. "We need to talk," he said in a stern tone.

Matt frowned. "Is there a problem?"

"I should say so," Professor Valentine replied. "Several students approached me just now to tell me that after I left the classroom at the beginning of the exam, they thought something was going on between you, James Potter, and another student."

Matt's jaw dropped. "Y-you think I was cheating?" he managed to sputter after a moment. "You know me. I don't cheat."

"I'm afraid that's not going to be good enough," Professor Valentine told him.

Rev. Camden opened the drawer and pulled out a handful of forks. "Four, five, six..." he counted.

Mrs. Camden was at the sink washing lettuce for a salad. "Make it seven," she called out to her husband. "Simon invited Lee Patterson for dinner again."

Lee Patterson. Grabbing an extra fork and closing the drawer, Rev. Camden's thoughts drifted to his earlier conversation with Sergeant Michaels. Lee had lied about his father's being a private investigator. But why? And what was Jeff Patterson's real story?

There was a soft, tentative knock at the

back door. Rev. Camden walked over and opened it.

It was Lee. He was dressed in the same jeans and hooded sweatshirt as yesterday, and he had a backpack slung over one shoulder.

"Hi, Reverend Camden. Mrs. Camden," Lee said with a smile.

"Hello, Lee," Rev. Camden said.

Mrs. Camden smiled at Lee. "Simon's upstairs. Dinner will be ready in just a bit." She added, "Hope you like lasagna."

"I *love* lasagna," Lee said eagerly.

Lee closed the door behind him. He started to shift his backpack from one shoulder to the other. But he lost his grip on it for a second, and it fell to the floor. The backpack's contents scattered everywhere.

Panic quickly flashed in Lee's eyes. He dropped to his knees and started picking up his stuff. Rev. Camden bent down to help.

"That's okay, I've got it," Lee said quickly.

"No problem, I'll give you a hand," Rev. Camden assured him. He picked up a book, a brush, a candy bar...and a clear plastic bag full of something that looked like dried oregano.

Rev. Camden took a closer look at the plastic bag.

"What's going on?" a voice asked from the top of the back stairs. It was Simon. He was headed down the stairs and into the kitchen, with Happy at his heels. Pausing at the bottom, Simon frowned in confusion at his father and Lee and the mess on the floor.

Rev. Camden rose slowly to his feet. Lee did, too. Rev. Camden then held the bag out to Lee.

"This is marijuana, isn't it?" he said grimly.

All the color had drained out of Lee's face. "I can explain!" he insisted.

"You can explain what a bag of marijuana is doing in your backpack?" Rev. Camden said skeptically.

Simon stared at Lee, his eyes wide with shock. And then he rushed up to his father. "Maybe he found it," he blurted out.

Rev. Camden turned to Lee, searching for the truth. However, he knew full well that Lee was likely to offer anything *but* the truth. Lee wouldn't look him in the eye. "I *did* find it," he murmured. "It's not mine, honest. I swear."

Rev. Camden then turned to Simon. He saw

Lee, either. Rev. Camden's heart went out to his son. And to Lee. He knew that getting to the truth, and to whatever healing might lie ahead, was going to be a very long and difficult road.

CHAPTER SEVEN

CRISIS

Mrs. Camden sat very still on the living room couch. Her eyes were fixed on a pretty figurine on the mantel, one her children had given her last Mother's Day. But she wasn't really seeing it. She wasn't really seeing anything at all.

"Annie?"

Her head jerked up. Her husband was hovering over her, looking concerned.

"Huh? I'm sorry. I was just..." She shook her head briskly, trying to make herself return to reality.

Rev. Camden sat down and put his arm around her. "Simon and Lee are upstairs," he told her quietly. "And Sergeant Michaels is on his way."

"Good. I don't want you going over to see

Lee's father by yourself," Mrs. Camden said, sucking in a deep breath. "Lee is only thirteen. How did this happen?"

"As scary as it seems, the facts say thirteen is the average age that most kids first try marijuana," Rev. Camden said.

Mrs. Camden thought about Lee: his shy smile, his soft voice. He and Simon eating pizza together, laughing, talking about the sort of stuff thirteen-year-old boys like to talk about. It just didn't make sense.

She turned to her husband. "But Lee, he seemed so…" She paused as she began to feel anger well up inside her. "We talk to our kids about drugs. Don't other people, too?" she cried out.

Rev. Camden shook his head. "Face it. We don't have to worry about some pusher on a city street. We have to worry about some kid offering one of *our* kids a joint during recess."

Then a terrible thought occurred to Mrs. Camden. "Do you think he offered Simon drugs?"

"No, I don't," Rev. Camden replied. "You saw Simon's face—it looked like he had no idea about the marijuana."

Mrs. Camden nodded, relieved.

Rev. Camden's gaze drifted upward. "Poor Simon. This is going to be very hard on him. He and Lee were starting to become good friends."

Upstairs, the two boys were sitting on Simon's bed. Simon was turning a baseball over and over in his hand. He and Lee hadn't said a word to each other since they'd been up there.

Finally, Simon set the baseball down on the bed. Without looking at Lee, he said, "The pot. You didn't find it, did you?"

"No," Lee admitted.

Simon stared at him. Lee leaned toward him and said in a whisper, "What I'm going to tell you, you can't tell anyone else."

Simon nodded mutely. He wasn't sure he was ready to hear this.

"The pot," Lee said. "It belongs to my dad."

Simon's jaw dropped. "Y-your dad?"

"Uh-huh," Lee said.

Simon thought about this. "I really do want to believe you," he said after a moment.

Lee's eyes welled up with tears. "I don't want to lose you as a friend," he said hoarsely.

"Please, you have to believe me."

Simon didn't respond. He wasn't sure what to believe anymore.

"No…no…*maybe*. Actually, no."

Lucy flung a red dress, and then a denim skirt, and then a blue silk shirt over her shoulder. She was going through each and every item in her closet. The floor behind her was littered with clothes. But Lucy didn't care. She was on a mission.

Ruthie breezed into the room, chomping on a wad of gum. She stopped in her tracks and stared at the mess. "Mary's not going to be happy," she announced to her sister. "You *do* share this room, you know?"

"Huh? Yeah, whatever." Lucy inspected a black velvet jumper and then flung that over her shoulder as well.

Ruthie plopped down on the bed and blew a big purple bubble. "What are you doing, anyway?" she asked, popping the bubble.

"I'm looking for an outfit to wear for a dance next week," Lucy explained. "But it's hopeless. Clearly, I have nothing to wear."

Ruthie had a sudden thought. Her eyes

gleamed. "I could help," she told her older sister.

Lucy regarded Ruthie suspiciously. "How?"

"I could get Mary to loan you her new pink sweater," Ruthie told her.

Lucy narrowed her eyes. "And what do you want in return?"

"Just the honor of being your sister," Ruthie said brightly.

Lucy gave her a look. Ruthie quickly added, "And maybe you could mow the lawn for Simon on Saturday."

"Okay, what are you up to?" Lucy asked.

"Just helping the people I love," Ruthie replied.

Lucy was used to Ruthie's schemes, and she knew that they usually meant trouble. *I probably shouldn't be having this discussion with her,* Lucy thought.

"You know, Mary will never say yes," Lucy pointed out. "The sweater cost fifty dollars, and she's never even worn it."

Then Lucy caught sight of the clothes all over the floor. She was running out of options. "On the other hand, it *would* look fabulous with my khaki mini-skirt..."

Ruthie's face lit up. "Okay, then?"

Lucy sighed. "Okay. Get me the sweater and I'll mow the lawn."

As Ruthie walked out of the room, Lucy could swear she heard her little sister say, *"Two down..."*

Matt was deep in thought. He couldn't figure out what to do about the James Potter situation. It was bad enough that James had cheated. But now *he* was accused of being a part of it.

How could this be happening? Matt wondered.

He opened the back door of his parents' house and walked into the kitchen. He had about twenty seconds to pick up his laundry, say hi, and leave, because he had to get back to campus right away. But as soon as he saw his parents' faces as they sat at the kitchen counter, he stopped in his tracks. "Hey. What's wrong?" he asked.

"Nothing," Rev. Camden replied.

Matt frowned. "Well, if that's what you guys look like when there's 'nothing' wrong, I'd hate to see what you look like in a crisis."

"We'll tell you later," his father assured him.

Matt nodded. "Good enough."

Mrs. Camden hugged her son. "How did your history midterm go?"

Matt sighed and pulled up a chair. He decided to take a minute and tell his parents what was going on. Besides, he knew that talking to them always made him feel better.

"Well, speaking of a crisis...do you know James Potter?" Matt said, sitting down.

"I know his father, Roy," Rev. Camden replied.

"Well, I hope he's nothing like his son," Matt remarked bitterly.

His parents stared at him. "What do you mean?" Mrs. Camden asked.

"I tried to help James. You know, tutor him for the midterm," Matt explained. "Then he cheated with this other guy during the test, and the professor thinks I'm involved, too."

"But you don't cheat," Rev. Camden said immediately.

"I know," Matt said. "Now all I have to do is convince Professor Valentine."

"What about the other boys?" his mother asked him, looking concerned.

Matt made a face. "From what I hear, James will probably have his dad fix it with the school. Apparently, he's a big contributor." His parents stared at him as he got up, walked over to the drier, and picked up his basket of laundry. "Hey, it could be worse," he said with a shrug. "According to the honor code I signed, the professor could have flunked me right on the spot."

Just then, the fuzzy, crackly sound of crying came over the baby monitor. Matt realized that David and Samuel must be waking up.

"You want me to get them?" he asked his parents.

Mrs. Camden shook her head and started upstairs. "No, I'll get them. Be right back."

Mrs. Camden took the back stairs up to the twins' room. When she got there, she saw Mary in the rocking chair, rocking David and Samuel.

Despite what had happened in the last hour—the shocking discovery about Lee, and then Matt's troubling news—Mrs. Camden couldn't help but melt at the sight of her oldest daughter with the baby twins. She took a deep breath and tried to let the good feeling wash over her to make some of the bad feelings go away.

"You're going to make a wonderful mother someday, Mary," she said softly.

Mary glanced up. "I don't know how you do it all. The babies, the five of us, Dad, shopping, cooking…"

"I have help," Mrs. Camden replied. "Motherhood is a lot of work, but it's also a blessing. A blessing I hope you have the good fortune to experience, when you're ready."

Mary's lips quivered ever so slightly. But it was just enough to set off Mrs. Camden's radar. "What's wrong?" she asked her daughter.

Mary stared at her. "How do you know something is wrong?"

"Another blessing of motherhood," Mrs. Camden replied.

Mary hesitated, then said, "There's a rumor going around school that Corey had a baby when she was fourteen."

"Do you think it's true?" Mrs. Camden asked her.

"I know it's true," Mary replied. "Corey told me. I met her daughter. I'm still a little blown away by it."

Mrs. Camden nodded. "Mrs. Conway, Corey's mom, told me about Corey two years ago."

Mary looked at her, stunned. *"What?"*

"She asked me not to tell anyone," Mrs. Camden explained. "After Corey had her baby, they moved to Glenoak to give Corey a fresh start so she could finish high school without having the whole town talking about her."

"Y-you knew?" Mary stammered.

"Mrs. Conway needed someone to talk to, someone she could trust," Mrs. Camden told her. "It's not easy when your fourteen-year-old daughter has a baby."

"I guess not," Mary agreed. She glanced down at her little brothers, who were cooing happily in her arms.

"Corey was lucky," Mrs. Camden went on. "When she got pregnant and needed help, her mother was there for her. But a lot of girls don't always find the love and support they need."

Mary got up from the rocking chair. She handed David to her mother and continued holding Samuel. "The whole school is talking about Corey. She's really upset by it."

Mrs. Camden kissed David on the head and

nodded. "People don't understand. Sometimes you can do more damage with words than with weapons."

Mary nodded sadly.

"Aww, come here, honey," Mrs. Camden said, putting her arm around Mary. Mary leaned into her, and they stood like that— mother, daughter, and two cooing babies—for a long, comforting moment.

Downstairs, Rev. Camden was talking to Sergeant Michaels in the kitchen. Matt had gone back to campus, and everyone else was upstairs.

The two men faced each other, their expressions grim.

"I did some checking," Sergeant Michaels said, taking his hat off.

Rev. Camden raised his eyebrows. "And?"

"Like I told you, Jeff Patterson has had some trouble with the law," Sergeant Michaels explained. "He was arrested two years ago for possession of marijuana. He plead it out and received probation. Then he and Lee moved in with his mother—Lee's grandmother—who currently holds down *two* jobs supporting the family. Her name is Marie Patterson."

Rev. Camden let the information sink in. "Is Lee's mother dead?" he asked after a moment.

Sergeant Michaels shook his head. "No, she's very much alive, or at least she was two years ago. She forfeited custody of Lee when he was five years old. Maybe it's easier for him to think of his mother as dead than as an addict who abandoned him."

Poor Lee, Rev. Camden thought. "Where is she now?" he asked the sergeant.

"No one knows," Sergeant Michaels replied. "Every once in a while, she shows up in a rehab clinic."

Rev. Camden took a deep breath. This was much worse than he had thought. It also explained a lot about Lee's behavior: his lying, the secrecy. The boy had grown up without love, stability, or boundaries, and without any real parents to speak of.

"I'll go upstairs and fetch Lee," Rev. Camden told Sergeant Michaels. "It's time we had a heart-to-heart with his father."

This was definitely not a conversation that Rev. Camden was looking forward to. But it was one that desperately needed to take place.

*   *   *

The phone jangled noisily. Upstairs in her room, Lucy picked it up. "Hello?"

"Hey, Lucy, it's Tyler."

Lucy's heart began beating like mad. *A visit and a phone call in one day! He must really, really like me,* she thought, overwhelmed.

Trying to sound cool, or at least not like a totally lovesick geek, she said, "Hey, Tyler. What's up?"

"I could use some help with something," Tyler said.

"Anything," Lucy told him eagerly.

"Well, I almost hate to ask."

"Ask, ask!"

Tyler hesitated for a second. "I have a C in biology this semester."

Lucy paused. She wondered where he was going with this. "And…?" she said.

"So I need access to the school's main computer to change my grade," Tyler explained. "Which, because of your new job in the attendance office, you can help me out with."

Lucy's jaw dropped. "I—I can't do that."

"You don't really have to do anything. Just give me the password to the school computer,"

Tyler said. "You can even leave the office. I'll do the rest."

Lucy couldn't believe what she was hearing. Was Tyler asking her to break the rules for him? For all she knew, it was even breaking the law! Before she could say anything, Tyler rushed on. "Look, my mom's calling me. We can talk about the details tomorrow at your sister's awards assembly. Good night, Lucy." With that, he hung up.

Lucy just sat there listening to the drone of the dial tone. *What on Earth just happened here?* she thought.

CHAPTER EIGHT

CONFRONTATIONS

The pool hall was bustling with the usual crowd. Waiters and waitresses hurried by with trays of sodas, and the smell of pizza filled the air. In the corner, the jukebox was playing loud, lively music.

Matt and Shana walked in and scanned the room for a table. She looped her arm through his and smiled up at him. "Dinner tonight is my treat," she told him.

"What, the condemned man gets a hearty last meal?" Matt joked.

"Ha ha," Shana said. And then her smile suddenly vanished.

"What?" Matt asked her curiously.

Shana pointed to the corner. James Potter

was sitting at a big table with a bunch of other students. They were all laughing about something.

Anger welled up inside of Matt. *That jerk,* he thought. *How dare he cheat on the exam, let his father get him off the hook, and then act like nothing ever happened!*

Shana turned to Matt. "Come on, let's go."

"No way," Matt said. He strode over to James, determined to have it out.

James glanced up as Matt approached his table. "Camden! Everyone, this is Matthew Camden, my personal tutor!"

Matt glared at James. "I hope you're happy," he hissed.

James folded his hands over his stomach and grinned. "I am. At this moment, my father is having a little chat with Professor Valentine. And when my father talks, people listen. Especially the little people." He added, "So unlike some of you, I don't think I'll be retaking the midterm."

Shana grabbed Matt's arm. "Come on, Matt, let's go," she insisted.

"If there's one thing I've learned from the old man, it's deny, deny, deny," James went on.

"Or is it lie, lie, lie? Oh, I forget...I get them confused."

Matt shook his head. *Just drop it*, he told himself. *James Potter is an immature idiot*. He started to walk off.

But then he heard James call after him: "Hey, Camden, why don't you get your old man to call God? Maybe the Big Guy can pull some strings for you."

James and his friends broke into loud laughter. Matt couldn't take it anymore. He whirled around and lunged at James.

"Matt, no!" Shana cried out. She put herself between Matt and James. "He's not worth it!"

Matt stopped, his hands clenched into fists. Shana was right. He took a few deep breaths, trying to regain his self-control.

"Come on, let's get out of here," he told her after a moment. He narrowed his eyes at James and added, "My dad taught me something, too...if you have a problem, go to the source."

James frowned. "Huh? What are you talking about?"

"You'll see," Matt told him. "You'll see."

Mary stood in front of her mother's dresser.

She opened the jewelry box and regarded its contents. Earrings, bracelets, necklaces, pins. Everything was so fancy and beautiful.

Mary lifted a pearl pendant, held it up to her neck, then put it back. She was looking for something that she might be able to borrow for the awards assembly tomorrow. She wanted to look especially good. Because despite the situation with Corey, it was still a big day for her.

Who knows? Mary thought. *Maybe by tomorrow, everyone will calm down and realize that Corey is still Corey. So she had a baby when she was fourteen,* Mary thought. *She's still the super-nice, super-smart, super-talented girl we all know, like, and admire.*

Mary held a pair of turquoise earrings up to her ears and gazed into the mirror. As she did, she caught a reflection of Ruthie standing in the doorway.

Mary turned around. Ruthie skipped into the room, plopped down on their parents' bed, and stared up at her older sister.

"What do you want?" Mary asked.

"I want to help you," Ruthie replied.

"Why does that scare me?" Mary said.

Ruthie got up and walked over to the

dresser. She scanned their mother's jewelry box, then pulled out a pair of sparkly antique earrings.

Ruthie held them up to Mary's ears. "You should wear *these* at the assembly tomorrow."

How did she know I was looking for something to wear at the assembly? Mary wondered. *Ruthie always seems to know everything.* "But Mom doesn't let anyone wear these," she told Ruthie. "They used to be Grandma's."

"I bet I can get Mommy to loan them to you," Ruthie told her confidently.

Mary started. "What? How?" She had to admit, she was curious. *Grandma's earrings would be absolutely perfect,* she thought.

Ruthie waved her hands dismissively. "Don't worry about that. Do you want to wear them or not?"

Mary regarded her skeptically. "Maybe...I don't know. What do I have to do in return?" She knew how her little sister operated—there was always something in return.

"Just loan Lucy your new pink sweater," Ruthie said.

Mary broke into laughter. "I really wish I knew what you're up to."

"I'm not up to anything," Ruthie said innocently. "So what do you say? Do we have a deal?"

"If I say yes, will you leave me alone?" Mary asked her.

Ruthie thought for a moment. "Sure."

"Then yes, Lucy can borrow my sweater," Mary agreed.

Ruthie rubbed her hands together. "Excellent."

As she walked out of the room, Mary could swear she heard her little sister say, *"Three down..."*

Mrs. Camden was finishing up the last of the dinner dishes when Simon came trotting down the back stairs. He glanced around the kitchen.

"Dad's not home yet?" he said with a frown.

Mrs. Camden shook her head. "No," she said.

Simon started to head back upstairs. But Mrs. Camden didn't want him to go. She wanted to talk to him, and hold him, and tell him that everything would be okay. She spotted the tray of oatmeal cookies on the kitchen table, the ones she'd baked that afternoon.

"Want a cookie?" she called after him hopefully.

Simon stopped and turned around. "Mom, I'm not five anymore. If you want to talk to me, just say you want to talk. You don't have to trick me into it by offering cookies."

Mrs. Camden hung her head. "Okay, Simon. I want to talk." She sat down at the table, and Simon pulled up the chair next to her and sat down, too. Mrs. Camden looked at him for a moment—her sweet, smart, beautiful son, who was all tied up in knots because his friend was in trouble with drugs. *Why does life have to be so hard and complicated sometimes?* she wondered.

She was about to speak, but she could tell that Simon wanted to say something. And so she waited until he gathered up enough courage to do so. After a long moment, Simon said, "Lee said the marijuana was his dad's. He uses it when he works with the police."

Mrs. Camden raised her eyebrows. "Do you believe him?"

Simon sighed. "I don't know."

Mrs. Camden took a deep breath. "You know, when someone wants to hide something badly enough, they can usually get away with it for a little while," she began. "But sooner or later, the truth comes out, and then you have to decide whether you're going to face it or deny it. For a lot of people, it's easier to deny that their friend, or a family member, is doing something wrong than to face the truth and take action."

Simon stared at her. "Life sure was a lot easier when I was younger," he said with a sad smile.

"I know, honey," Mrs. Camden said wistfully. "You want a cookie?"

Simon nodded as Mrs. Camden handed him a cookie. Then she reached over and hugged him, wishing that she could make all his pain—and *everyone's* pain—go away.

Rev. Camden walked up the Pattersons' driveway with a heavy heart. Sergeant Michaels was right behind him, followed by Lee. It was a cold, dark night with no moon or stars in the sky.

Rev. Camden knew Lee was really scared. In fact, the poor boy had been silent the whole ride over. But Rev. Camden also knew this conversation had to take place. They had to talk to his father and tell him what was going on.

The garage door was open. Inside the garage was a gray-haired woman dressed in a waitress's uniform. She was standing in front of an old, dented washer, folding clothes with a weary expression on her face.

This must be Marie Patterson, Lee's grandmother, Rev. Camden thought.

Mrs. Patterson noticed the three of them coming up the driveway. She set the laundry down. "What's going on? Is everything okay?"

Rev. Camden stepped forward. "I'm Reverend Eric Camden, Simon's father. And this is Sergeant Michaels from the Glenoak Police Department. We need to talk to you about something that happened at my house tonight."

"What? What happened?" asked Mrs. Patterson.

"Lee had a bag full of marijuana in his backpack," Rev. Camden continued.

Mrs. Patterson looked surprised. But not too surprised, Rev. Camden noticed.

"Lee?" Mrs. Patterson said, her eyebrows raised. "Is this true?"

Before Lee could say anything, a door at the back of the garage burst open, and a man stepped out. He was of medium height and dark-haired. He was dressed in a dirty T-shirt and jeans.

"What's all the racket?" the man demanded irritably.

Mrs. Patterson nodded at Rev. Camden. "Jeff, this man says he found drugs on Lee," she said pointedly.

Mr. Patterson shrugged. "Well, he didn't get them from me," he quickly said in defense.

Rev. Camden and Sergeant Michaels exchanged a glance. Jeff Patterson noticed this and descended on his son with a furious expression. "Did you tell them they were *my* drugs?" he asked. "Is that what this is all about? Cause you people should know he's a little liar, my son. Isn't that right, Lee? You like to make up stories about everything. Don'tcha?"

"I didn't say I got it from you, Dad, I swear," Lee said in a trembling voice. "I told them I *found* it."

He turned to Rev. Camden with a desperate expression. "It's not my dad's marijuana. You have to believe me!"

Rev. Camden sighed. He was beginning to understand the situation all too well. "Look," he said patiently to Mr. Patterson. "I'm a minister at the Glenoak church. And if there's a problem, I can help. I can—"

Mr. Patterson waved his hand dismissively. "That's nice, but I think you should mind your own business."

"When your son brought drugs into my house, it *became* my business," Rev. Camden told him firmly.

Mr. Patterson narrowed his eyes at Sergeant Michaels. "Are you going to arrest Lee?"

Sergeant Michaels shook his head. "No, but I am going to file a report."

"File anything you want, but leave me, my son, and my mother alone," Mr. Patterson snapped. With that, he pulled his mother and Lee inside the house and slammed the door.

CHAPTER NINE

DO THE RIGHT THING

The morning sun was shining brightly through the kitchen window. It was going to be a beautiful day for the assembly, Mary thought. She'd even managed to write most of her speech before she went to bed last night. *Maybe everything's going to be okay, after all,* she told herself. She gulped down some orange juice and then finished off the rest of her cereal. She was just about to get up from the table when Lucy walked in.

She sat down at the table next to Mary. Mary could tell that her younger sister was worried about something.

"Okay, what?" Mary asked her.

"A very cute guy asked me to the Fall Fling dance," Lucy began.

Mary shrugged. "So?"

"He also asked me to give him the password to the school's main computer so he can alter his school records."

Mary put her spoon down and stared at her sister.

"What? What are you thinking?" Lucy said, looking worried.

"You're not stupid," Mary told her sternly. "You know the difference between right and wrong. You also know that anyone who would ask you to do that is not someone you need to be dating."

Lucy nodded quickly. "You're right. I know."

"Duh," Mary said.

"I just needed some extra support," Lucy told her, smiling weakly. "It's not every day you tell Tyler Smith to get lost."

"Tyler Smith!" Mary said in amazement. "Tyler Smith is dating Courtney Webber. They're practically married."

"Tyler said they broke up," Lucy said meekly.

Mary rolled her eyes. "Oh my gosh, color me surprised, a guy who asked you to help him break into the school computer *lied*."

Just then, the phone rang. Lucy got up and walked across the room to answer it.

"Hello? Sure. Just a sec." Lucy walked back to the table. "It's Corey," she said, covering the mouthpiece. "She sounds, um…kind of upset."

Mary frowned and took the phone from her sister. "Corey? What's going on?"

Upstairs in her room, Mrs. Camden was having a hard time deciding what to wear. Her thoughts were in disarray. There was so much going on—Lee and his father, Matt being falsely accused of cheating, and Corey Conway's situation. Still, she wanted to look nice for Mary's assembly. She knew this was a big day for her daughter.

She heard a little coughing noise behind her: *ah-hem*. She turned around. Ruthie was standing in the doorway. She was watching her mother with a big grin on her face.

Mrs. Camden knew that look. "What?" she said suspiciously.

Ruthie shook her head. "I shouldn't."

Mrs. Camden's mouth curled up into a smile. "Shouldn't…what?"

"Well," Ruthie said with a dramatic sigh. "I

overheard Mary telling Lucy how much she wanted to wear Grandma's sparkle earrings to the assembly today."

Mrs. Camden lit up. "Really?"

Ruthie nodded. "It would mean the *world* to her."

Minutes later, still dressed in her jeans and sweatshirt, Mrs. Camden walked out into the hallway with her mother's antique earrings in hand. She ran into Mary coming up the stairs.

"Just the Camden I was looking for!" Mrs. Camden said brightly. "I thought maybe you'd like to wear Grandma's earrings to the assembly today." And then she noticed the grim expression on Mary's face. "What's wrong?" Mrs. Camden asked her.

"Corey just called," Mary told her. "They're taking away her half of the award because they found out she had a baby. They think giving her the award would endorse teen pregnancy." She added bitterly, "I'm not going. I don't *want* their stupid award!"

Mrs. Camden shook her head. *How can people be so narrow-minded?* she wondered.

But then Mrs. Camden had an idea. "I've

got a better plan. In fact, it's a perfect plan. Mary, how fast can you rewrite your acceptance speech?"

Rev. Camden was standing at the refrigerator. He was trying to decide between eating a grapefruit half and somebody's leftover blueberry muffin when he heard a soft knock at the back door.

Now who could that be? he wondered.

It was Lee. A very shaken-up-looking Lee.

Rev. Camden drew the boy inside and shut the door. "What's wrong?" he asked, concerned. "What happened?"

"I—I ran away," Lee admitted. He set his backpack down on the kitchen table and glanced up at Rev. Camden. The reverend saw that his eyes were shiny with tears. "I lied last night...the marijuana belongs to my dad."

Rev. Camden nodded. "I know."

Lee looked stunned. "Y-you know?" he said slowly.

"I figured it out," Rev. Camden told him.

Lee was silent for a moment. Then he continued. "After my grandmother left for work last night, my dad started yelling at me. He's mad about me bringing the police and you over to the house, and he's really upset about me losing his drugs. My grandmother is still at work. I didn't know where else to go."

"You came to the right place, Lee," a voice said in the background.

Rev. Camden turned around and saw Simon standing at the bottom of the stairs.

Lee went up to Simon. "You're still my friend?" he said, sounding surprised.

Simon nodded.

"But I lied to you," Lee said, hanging his head.

"You only have to do two things to be my friend," Simon told him. "Don't lie any-more...and stay away from drugs."

Lee smiled gratefully. "I can definitely do that."

Reverend Camden beamed at his son. He was incredibly proud of him at the moment.

"Simon," he said. "Take Lee upstairs and finish getting ready. He can come with us to Mary's assembly."

"Reverend Camden?" Lee spoke up.

The reverend raised his eyebrows. "Yes?"

Lee smiled again. "Thanks."

Rev. Camden nodded. As the boys headed upstairs, he picked up the phone. Then he dialed what was becoming an all-too-familiar number. "Sergeant Michaels, please."

After a moment, the sergeant came on the line. "Sergeant Michaels here."

"It's Eric Camden. Lee Patterson ran away, but he's over here."

"Well, at least we know he's safe," Sergeant Michaels said with a sigh.

"Yes, but..." Rev. Camden said as he clenched his fists in frustration. "We know the drugs belong to his father. And we're positive that he's still using. Can we go in there and arrest him?"

"It's not that easy," the sergeant replied. "If we arrest him for possession, Lee would have to testify against his father."

"What about the grandmother?" Rev. Camden persisted.

"I think she's in deep denial about her son. If I get Social Services involved, they'll get Lee out of the house, but they'll also put him in foster care."

Rev. Camden hesitated. "I want to do what's in Lee's best interest. But I don't think that's foster care."

"Agreed."

"I think what Lee's father needs is a shove in the right direction and a little motivation to straighten up his life," Rev. Camden said.

There was a moment of silence on the line. Then Sergeant Michaels said, "Do you want to be the shove or the motivation?"

"The motivation," Rev. Camden said immediately.

Sergeant Michaels chuckled somberly. "I guess that makes me the shove."

"It's a plan," Rev. Camden agreed.

Matt walked into Professor Valentine's classroom and sat down in the front row. There was no one else there. He glanced at the faded chalk writing on the blackboard that said: AMERICAN HISTORY MIDTERM TODAY. He shuddered at the memory of the exam, wishing that he could live yesterday all over again.

There's still some hope, he thought. He'd had a conversation last night after he dropped Shana off at her house—a conversation that just might settle everything.

Matt glanced at his watch: ten after nine. He had gotten a message from James Potter asking him to meet him at nine. *I wonder what*

James wants? he wondered.

At that moment, James strolled into the room. Matt instantly felt anger rise up in him. He had to tell himself: *Calm down, take a deep breath, and don't get into it with him.* "Okay, so, what do you want?" he asked James.

"I was just about to ask *you* that, Camden," James replied, looking puzzled. "I got a message to meet you here."

Matt was totally confused. "Huh? But I got a message to meet *you* here."

Just then, a tall, well-dressed, middle-aged man walked into the room. James stared at him. "Dad?" he blurted out. And then he stared at Matt. "What's going on?" he demanded.

"Sit down, James," Mr. Potter ordered.

James opened his mouth but then clamped it shut. He sat down at a nearby desk and slumped way down in the chair. Mr. Potter crossed the room and extended a hand to Matt. "Roy Potter. You must be Matt Camden."

Matt clasped Mr. Potter's hand. Then Mr. Potter turned to his son and said, "I spoke with Matt last night on the phone. He told me a very interesting story."

"Well, he's lying," James said coolly.

Mr. Potter shook his head. "I don't think so."

James made a face. "Dad…come on…" he moaned.

Mr. Potter gazed at his son for a long moment. "I'm sorry."

"It's okay, I'm sure Matt was pretty convincing," James said, beginning to sound angry.

Mr. Potter shook his head again. "No, James. I'm sorry for every problem of yours that I solved, and every university that I bought you into. I'm sorry for giving you too much too soon. I'm sorry for giving you everything—but really giving you nothing."

James looked stunned. "*What* are you talking about?"

"I'm going to call Professor Valentine, but not to bail you out," Mr. Potter told his son. "I'm going to let him know that he should reconsider punishing Matt, whose only mistake was trying to help you out."

James threw up his hands. "I—I can't believe this!" he sputtered.

"Before it's too late, you need to figure out how to get through life on your own two feet," Mr. Potter declared. "I know it won't be today, but someday you're going to thank me for doing this.

"I'm sorry for any problems my son might have caused you," Mr. Potter then told Matt.

"No apology necessary," Matt replied. Then he leaned back in his seat, letting relief wash over him.

Crisis over.

CHAPTER TEN

THE ASSEMBLY

The hallway outside of the high school auditorium was bustling with students, parents, and teachers. Many of them were more dressed up than usual in honor of the big awards assembly.

Lucy was standing around, looking very nice in her red sweater and denim skirt. Suddenly, she felt a tap on her shoulder and turned around. It was Tyler Smith, looking gorgeous as usual. He was smiling his perfect smile at her.

Amazing, Lucy thought. *That smile does nothing for me anymore.*

"Hey," Tyler said.

"Hello," Lucy replied coldly.

Tyler leaned closer to her. "So, what's a good

day to do that computer thing we talked about?" he asked her.

Lucy pretended to think for a moment. "Um, how about…never?"

Tyler looked startled. "What?"

Lucy shook her head. "I thought I knew better."

"But you said you were going to help me out," Tyler insisted.

Lucy glared at him. "I knew you were still dating Courtney, but I was willing to deny the truth. Unfortunately, when you asked me to break into the school computer, I kind of woke up and realized you were using me."

Tyler stopped smiling. Lucy could see that he was floundering around for a new strategy. "I—I still think you're real pretty," he said.

As if that's going to make me change my mind, Lucy thought irritably. Thinking quickly, she smiled at him and said, "That is *so* sweet. I think you're pretty, too…*pretty sleazy.* Bye-bye now!"

Lucy waved at him. Tyler just stared at her, then stormed off in a huff.

Score one for me, Lucy thought.

*   *   *

Ruthie walked through the double doors of the high school, accompanied by her parents, Mary, Simon, and Simon's friend Lee. Ruthie looped her hand through her father's arm.

"I found a way to pay for my walkie-talkies," she told him.

Rev. Camden looked surprised. "Really?"

Ruthie grinned triumphantly. "Yeah. And I didn't have to do any work!"

Behind her, Ruthie heard her mother whisper to Mary, "I took care of everything."

"Good," Ruthie heard Mary whisper back.

Ruthie turned around. *What are these two talking about, anyway? What are they taking care of?* she thought.

She opened her mouth to ask. But before she could say anything, she saw something very disturbing.

Mary's ears were...totally bare. No earrings!

"You're not wearing Grandma's sparkle earrings," Ruthie said anxiously.

Mary shrugged. "They didn't go with my outfit."

"Hey, guys!" Lucy called from behind them. She was weaving through a crowd of people, making her way toward them.

Ruthie gulped. How was she going to tell Lucy that she probably couldn't count on Mary's pink sweater anymore? And, more importantly, how would she still get her to mow the lawn for Simon on Saturday?

Lucy paused in front of Ruthie. "By the way, I don't need to borrow your pink sweater," she said cheerfully to Mary. "I no longer have a date to the dance."

"Way to go, Sis," Mary told her, giving her a high-five.

Ruthie frowned. Why was Lucy acting happy about *not* having a date to the dance? And worse yet, what was happening to her plan? It was unraveling by the minute.

"This is not good," she muttered to herself.

"Oh, which means that I won't be mowing the lawn on Saturday, Ruthie," Lucy told her younger sister.

Simon then tapped Ruthie on the shoulder. "No lawn mowing, no loan."

"Which means no walkie-talkies," Ruthie said, sighing.

"Don't you think it would have been easier to just take out the trash?" her father asked her with a twinkle in his eye.

"I don't like it when you're right," Ruthie said glumly.

"We should probably go in and take our seats," Mrs. Camden announced, glancing at her watch. "Mary needs to get backstage."

Matt and Shana came running up at that moment. "Did we miss it?" Matt said breathlessly.

"No, you're just in time," Rev. Camden told him.

Ruthie slipped her hand into Shana's and smiled up at her. Ruthie really liked Shana— she was nice, friendly, and always thinking of other people…

"Hey, Ruthie," Shana said warmly. "How's it going?"

"Okay, I guess," Ruthie replied. "Hey, do you have twenty-nine dollars and ninety-nine cents I could borrow?"

As they took their seats inside the auditorium, Rev. Camden leaned over to Matt. "What happened with James Potter?" he said in a low voice.

Matt settled down in his seat. "Professor Valentine called me this morning," he began.

"That's why Shana and I were late. I don't have to retake the midterm. James told him I wasn't cheating."

Rev. Camden nodded. He was incredibly relieved. "Good. Very good."

"I guess when James realized that his dad wasn't going to bail him out again, his best bet was to tell the truth and throw himself on the mercy of the court," Matt went on. "Or the mercy of the professor, in this particular case."

"I'm glad things worked out," Rev. Camden told him.

Matt grinned at him. "By the way, Dad. When I called Mr. Potter last night, he told me you had called, too."

Rev. Camden started. *"You* called Roy Potter, too?"

Matt nodded.

Rev. Camden felt a rush of pride. "A chip off the old block," he said, putting his arm around Matt.

The principal, Ms. Russell, walked up to the podium and tapped on the microphone. Rev. Camden, Matt, and everyone else in the audience fell silent.

"Could everyone please take their seats?

We'd like to begin," she announced.

After everyone was settled, she continued. "Thank you. Today at the Glenoak High School All Sports Award Assembly, we're honoring the achievements of one of our standout seniors. A student who has always excelled in both sports and schoolwork. A student I will definitely be sorry to say good-bye to. I know you all know who I am talking about. So, without further ado, I'd like to announce this year's 'All Sports Award' recipient, Mary Camden!"

Rev. Camden watched proudly as Mary came out from backstage and went up to the podium. The auditorium erupted with applause. Ms. Russell handed Mary the award and shook her hand.

"Yay, Mary!" Ruthie shouted above the applause. "That's my sister, everybody!"

Rev. Camden felt his wife reach for his hand and squeeze it tight. He glanced over at her. To his surprise, she wasn't smiling. In fact, she was staring at Mary and looking very anxious. Rev. Camden wanted to ask her what was wrong, but he didn't get a chance. The applause died down, and Mary started speaking.

"I'd really like to thank the local businessmen's association for this honor," Mary began.

She hesitated. "But…I can't."

Rev. Camden sat up, surprised. People in the audience began buzzing in confusion.

"What is she talking about?" Matt whispered to him. "Why can't she accept the award?"

"I'm not sure," Rev. Camden whispered back.

Mary glanced down at the award. "'For excellence in sports and in life, to individuals we hope future generations see as role models,'" she read slowly. "I've never thought of myself as a role model. I go to school and get good grades. I go to basketball games and score points. But a role model? I don't think so."

She looked out at the audience. "There *was* a role model who was supposed to receive this award with me today. But at the last minute, the committee changed their minds. You all know who I'm talking about, because for the past twenty-four hours, most of you have done nothing but talk about her. She's my teammate and my friend. She's Corey Conway. And when she was fourteen, she had a baby."

Now the audience was *really* buzzing. Rev.

Camden turned and stared at his wife. She was smiling at Mary and nodding encouragingly. Clearly, she had known about this all along.

"Corey Conway is a *person,* not an issue," Mary went on, her voice sure and strong. "And the only endorsement that would be made by celebrating *her* achievements is to honor someone who didn't take the easy road in life. She did what few others could have done—finish high school, with honors, while raising a baby. I wanted you all to know how I felt before I brought Corey onstage and gave her my award. Because even though she's not a role model for the local businessmen's association, or for some of the students at this school…she is for me."

Mary paused and nodded toward backstage. A moment later, Corey Conway, Mrs. Conway, and Bernadette—Corey's daughter—walked onto the stage.

Mary extended her award to Corey. "For excellence in sports and in life," she pronounced.

Corey took the award from Mary, and the two girls embraced in a long hug. There was dead silence in the auditorium. Mary broke from the hug, smiled at Corey, and then began clapping. For a brief moment, she was the only one in the whole room who was doing so.

Then all the rest of the Camdens joined in.

Then, in the front row, Mary's teammate Elaine joined in, too. She even stood up.

Before long, the entire audience was on its feet, clapping and cheering wildly. And tears were streaming down Corey Conway's face.

CHAPTER ELEVEN

FAMILY REUNITED

I hope this works, Rev. Camden thought nervously, glancing at the faces around the living room.

He was sitting on the Camdens' living room couch, along with Mrs. Camden and Lee. Lee's grandmother, Marie Patterson, was sitting on a chair across from them. No one was talking. Everyone seemed incredibly anxious about what was about to happen.

The front door opened. Sergeant Michaels walked in, followed by Mr. Patterson.

Mr. Patterson stopped in his tracks and stared at the people in the room. "Okay," he said suspiciously. "What's going on?"

Rev. Camden stood up and stepped forward. "Your mother and son asked me to help them, Jeff. This is an intervention. Do you know what that is?"

Mr. Patterson shook his head in disgust and started walking back to the door. "I'm out of here."

Sergeant Michaels stepped in front of him, cutting him off. "You can either listen to your family, or you can go to jail. The choice is yours."

"I am not going to jail," Mr. Patterson protested.

"Marijuana possession is a direct violation of your parole," the sergeant informed him. "And that means some serious jail time."

Jeff Patterson turned to Lee. But before he could say anything to his son, Sergeant Michaels said, "Don't look at him. He's not going to lie for you anymore."

Mr. Patterson scanned the room. His face fell in defeat. "All right," he said wearily, sinking down into a chair. "You win. I'll listen."

No one said anything for a few minutes. Finally, Mr. Patterson spoke up. "I don't know what Lee told you. But I don't smoke pot. I used to, but I quit. You can ask anyone."

Lee got up and walked over to his father.

"Dad…" he said softly.

His father frowned at him. "Yeah?"

"Stop lying. Please just stop lying and stop making promises that you'll never keep," Lee said, his voice growing emotional. "I am so sick of all the lies. You smoke marijuana, and you know you do. Grandma knows you do, I know you do…and you know the marijuana that Reverend Camden found in my backpack is yours." Lee looked down at the ground, holding back tears. "I took it from you because I'm afraid if I left it at home, you'd smoke it and do something stupid," he said as his eyes brimmed with tears and his lips trembled. Mrs. Camden rushed over and put her arms around him.

Marie Patterson looked at her son. "I should have kicked you out. I should have told you that if you do drugs, then you can't live with me. But I thought turning my back on my only son would make me a bad mother." She shook her head bitterly. "I was wrong. It made me a bad grandmother."

"Mom…" Mr. Patterson said in a pleading tone.

But his mother wouldn't let him talk. "Look, if you won't straighten up for me, do it for Lee," she continued. "He's your son, and you should act like his father. If you don't make me a promise right here and now that you will take steps to clean up your life, I will get custody of Lee, and you will never see us again. I don't want to do it, but I can't sit by and watch my grandson turn to drugs like my son did."

Mother and son just stared at each other for a long, painful moment. Then Mr. Patterson turned to Rev. Camden, looking completely lost. His family's words were obviously having a major effect on him.

"Admitting you have a problem is the first step," Rev. Camden told him gently. "And I think it's the hardest step, too."

"I'll be there for you every step of the way," Marie Patterson told her son. "And as long as you stay clean and sober, you can live with me. But you're going to have to get a job and start contributing to the household."

Mr. Patterson stared at the floor and shook his head. "I just don't know if I can do it."

Lee turned to his father. "Dad, please," he begged. "I already lost a mom. I don't want to lose you, too. I...I love you."

Lee reached out to hug his father. His father

hugged him back, his eyes welling with tears.

"What do you say, Jeff?" Rev. Camden said quietly.

Mr. Patterson wiped the tears from his eyes and looked at his son. "I say that I have a problem. I need help...and I don't want to lose my son."

Simon was in his room trying to concentrate on his algebra homework. But he couldn't because he knew what was happening downstairs. He could hear the blur of voices coming up from the living room, but he couldn't tell what was actually being said. He had no idea if things were going well, or not so well...

Suddenly, there was a soft knock on the door. Simon's head shot up. "Come in!" he called.

It was his father. Simon looked at him expectantly. "Well? Did your plan work?"

"Perfectly," Rev. Camden assured him. "Lee's dad has a long road ahead of him, and so does Lee. But they've just made a very positive start."

Simon smiled. He was incredibly happy and relieved. "Thanks, Dad. Thanks for everything," he said, reaching out to give him a big hug. "It's a lucky thing Ruthie's not around— I'm in such a good mood now, I might even loan her that twenty-nine dollars and ninety-nine cents!"

"Don't get her started," Rev. Camden said, smiling.

DON'T MISS THESE
7TH HEAVEN BOOKS!

There's always a beginning...

With a "Meet the Stars" bonus section and 8 pages of color photos!

NOBODY'S PERFECT

Matt has his eye on a new girl, Lucy's trying out for cheerleading—with Mary trying to stop her— Simon's attempting to become invisible, and Ruthie's scrambling just to keep up. Welcome to America's favorite TV family!

MARY'S STORY

Big sis Mary seems to have it all together: She's practical, super-smart, beautiful, vivacious, and a rising star on her school's basketball team. But beneath her perfect exterior, sixteen-year-old Mary is struggling to figure out boys, friends, parents, and life in general—not to mention her younger sister Lucy!

Available wherever books are sold!
ISBN: 0-375-80332-7

MATT'S
STORY

As the oldest kid in the Camden clan and a college freshman, handsome eighteen-year-old Matt often bears the burden of playing referee between his siblings and his parents. Sometimes it's tough to balance family loyalty against a fierce desire for independence, but Matt has earned his reputation as the "responsible one"—*most* of the time.

Available wherever books are sold!
0-375-80333-5

RIVALS

For better or for worse, Mary and Lucy Camden have one thing in common: they're the oldest sisters in a *huge*, busy family! But sometimes the two of them hardly seem related: strong, independent Mary hangs out on the basketball court, while sensitive, impulsive Lucy loves the mall. And when there's a cute guy involved, it's all-out war!

Available wherever books are sold!
ISBN: 0-375-80337-8

MIDDLE SISTER

Sometimes being the middle girl in a big family is a tight squeeze—just ask Lucy Camden! It can be kind of tough when your older sister is a beautiful, popular basketball star and your adorable younger sister has a knack for getting her own way. Dealing with brothers isn't always easy, either. But Lucy is her own person and she's determined to stand out—no matter what!

Available wherever books are sold!
ISBN: 0-375-80336-X

MR. NICE GUY

Simon Camden never gives up. When he wants something, he goes for it, no matter how much work (or begging!) it takes. Sometimes his brother and sisters get in the way, and often he feels as if his dog, Happy, is the only one who understands him. But despite his ambition, Simon is the first to help anyone in distress, even if it means putting some of his big plans on hold...

Available wherever books are sold!
ISBN: 0-375-80338-6

SECRETS

Everyone in the Camden household—maybe in the whole world—knows when something is troubling Lucy. She's always been the first in the family to speak up—until now...

Available wherever books are sold!
ISBN: 0-375-80340-8